THE FORGOTTEN ENCLAVE
BY LYLE DAVENPORT

The Forgotten Enclave

Lyle Davenport

Published by Am I Am, 2024.

This is a work of fiction. Similarities to real people, places, or events are entirely coincidental.

THE FORGOTTEN ENCLAVE

First edition. June 15, 2024.

Copyright © 2024 Lyle Davenport.

ISBN: 979-8227688125

Written by Lyle Davenport.

CONTENTS:

CHAPTER ONE

In the year 2137, the world as we knew it ended. A series of cataclysmic events, from devastating nuclear wars to widespread pandemics and natural disasters, shattered the fragile fabric of society. The once bustling cities, the centers of human civilization, lay in ruins, their skeletons crumbling under the weight of time and neglect. The remnants of humanity had retreated into isolated, self-sustaining enclaves, each one a tiny bastion of life in a vast, desolate wasteland.

These enclaves, scattered across the remnants of the world, were like islands in an ocean of desolation. Each one was a small, self-contained ecosystem, designed to be self-sufficient in the harshest of conditions. The people within these enclaves had little to no knowledge of the existence of others, and communication between them was nearly impossible due to the vast, treacherous expanses of wasteland that lay between them.

The enclave known as Bastion was nestled in the ruins of what was once a great metropolis. The towering skyscrapers that had once defined the city's skyline were now crumbling husks, their windows shattered, and their steel frames twisted and rusting. The streets were choked with debris and overgrown with weeds, the only signs of life being the occasional scurrying of small animals or the distant howls of wild dogs.

Inside Bastion, life had adapted to the new reality. The enclave was protected by high walls made of salvaged materials, reinforced with whatever could be found in the ruins. The inhabitants had learned to grow their own food in small, makeshift gardens, using every inch of available space. They had created rudimentary water filtration systems to purify the rainwater that was often contaminated by the fallout from the old wars. Power was generated by a mix of solar panels and hand-cranked generators, providing just enough electricity for the basic needs of the community.

The people of Bastion were a hardy lot, survivors who had endured unimaginable hardships. They had learned to live with the constant threat of raiders, bands of lawless scavengers who roamed the wastelands in search of easy prey. The walls of Bastion were manned day and night by sentries, always vigilant, always ready to repel any attack. The enclave had developed a strict code of conduct, a set of rules and regulations that everyone was expected to follow. Resources were scarce, and everything was rationed carefully. There was no room for waste or selfishness; the survival of the community depended on the cooperation and discipline of its members.

Beyond the walls of Bastion, the wasteland stretched out as far as the eye could see. The landscape was a grim tableau of destruction, dotted with the remnants of the old world. Rusting vehicles lay abandoned on cracked and overgrown highways. The skeletal remains of long-dead trees stood like mournful sentinels, their branches bare and lifeless. The air was thick with dust and the lingering scent of decay, a constant reminder of the world's fall from grace.

In the distance, the horizon was dominated by the looming shape of the Dark Mountain, a massive peak that had once been a dormant volcano. During the cataclysm, it had erupted violently, spewing ash and molten rock into the sky, and covering the land in a thick layer of soot. The mountain was now a symbol of the world's destruction, a stark reminder of the forces that had torn civilization apart.

Far to the south, another enclave, known as Haven, clung to existence. Haven was situated in what had once been a fertile valley, now transformed into a harsh, arid desert. The people of Haven had become expert water scavengers, extracting every drop of moisture from the parched earth. They had constructed a network of underground reservoirs and irrigation systems, using ancient techniques combined with whatever modern technology they could salvage.

Haven was a place of contrasts. Its people lived in simple adobe huts, built to withstand the searing heat of the day and the freezing cold of the night. They wore clothing made from animal hides and woven fibers, and their diet consisted mainly of drought-resistant crops and the occasional meat from small game. Despite the harsh conditions, Haven had a certain rugged beauty, with its stark landscapes and the resilient spirit of its inhabitants.

Life in Haven was centered around the oasis, a small but vital source of water that had miraculously survived the cataclysm. The oasis was carefully tended, its precious water guarded jealously. The people of Haven had developed a deep reverence for water, seeing it as a sacred gift that sustained their lives. Their rituals and ceremonies often revolved around the oasis, celebrating the cycles of nature and the resilience of their community.

To the east, another enclave known as Sanctuary had carved out a precarious existence in the shadow of a massive, crumbling dam. The dam had once held back a mighty river, providing water and power to the surrounding region. Now, it was a looming monolith of concrete and steel, its once-strong structure weakened by decades of neglect and the relentless forces of nature.

Sanctuary had managed to harness the remnants of the river, creating a series of small, interconnected ponds and streams that provided water for their crops and livestock. The people of Sanctuary were skilled engineers and craftsmen, adept at repairing and maintaining the dam's ancient machinery. They had managed to restore a small portion of the dam's power-generating capacity, giving them a precious source of electricity.

The inhabitants of Sanctuary lived in sturdy stone houses, built to withstand the frequent earthquakes and landslides that plagued the region. They had developed a system of tunnels and underground bunkers, providing shelter from the unpredictable weather and the occasional attacks from raiders. Sanctuary was a place of constant vigilance and hard work, but it was also a place of ingenuity and resourcefulness.

In the far north, the enclave known as Frostholm struggled against the relentless cold. Situated in the remains of a once-thriving industrial city, Frostholm was a place of perpetual winter, where snow and ice covered the ground year-round. The people of Frostholm had adapted to the freezing temperatures, building insulated shelters and learning to hunt and trap the hardy wildlife that roamed the frozen wasteland.

Frostholm's inhabitants were a close-knit community, bound together by the harsh conditions they faced. They had developed a unique way of life, relying on geothermal energy from the hot springs that dotted the region. The hot springs provided not only warmth but also a source of clean, hot water, which was used for cooking, bathing, and even heating their homes.

The people of Frostholm were skilled hunters and fishers, their diet consisting mainly of game and fish, supplemented by hardy root vegetables and grains that could withstand the cold. They wore thick furs and leather clothing, their faces often obscured by fur-lined hoods and scarves. Despite the isolation and the bitter cold, the community of Frostholm had a strong sense of identity and pride, their resilience a testament to the indomitable spirit of humanity.

As the years passed, the enclaves continued to endure, each one a microcosm of human adaptability and survival. The world outside their walls remained a hostile and unforgiving place, a barren wasteland where the remnants of the old world lay in silent decay. The skies were often darkened by clouds of ash and dust, and the air was thick with the scent of desolation.

The people of the enclaves had little to no knowledge of each other's existence, their lives shaped by the unique challenges and resources of their respective environments. They had become masters of their own small worlds, each enclave a testament to the human capacity for resilience and ingenuity in the face of unimaginable adversity.

Yet, the isolation and the constant struggle for survival had taken their toll. The people of the enclaves had grown wary and suspicious, their trust limited to those within their own walls. The idea of a larger, interconnected world had faded into myth and legend, replaced by the harsh realities of day-to-day existence. The dream of rebuilding a unified society seemed as distant and unattainable as the stars in the night sky.

In the end, the enclaves stood as silent witnesses to the fall of civilization, their inhabitants the last vestiges of a world that had once been vibrant and full of promise. The future was uncertain, and the past a distant memory, but within the walls of each enclave, life continued, a fragile flame flickering in the darkness of a post-apocalyptic world.

The sun, a swollen, sickly orange orb, cast long shadows over the barren expanse that was once a thriving world. The air was thick with dust and the acrid stench of decay, a lingering reminder of the cataclysm that had reduced cities to rubble and left the landscape a desolate wasteland. Scavengers moved like ghosts through the ruins, their eyes hollow and their bodies gaunt, driven by the unyielding hunger that gnawed at their bellies and their souls.

Cracked highways, once arteries of commerce and travel, lay strewn with the rusted carcasses of vehicles. Some were overturned, others were burned-out husks, their charred skeletons a testament to the inferno that had swept through. Weeds and hardy scrub pushed through the fissures in the asphalt, nature's tentative reclamation of what humanity had forsaken.

In the distance, the remnants of a city loomed, skeletal skyscrapers clawing at the sky, their glassy facades shattered and gaping. Concrete and steel, once symbols of progress and civilization, now stood as stark monuments to hubris and destruction. The silence was oppressive, broken only by the occasional gust of wind that sent eddies of dust swirling, whispering through the ruins like the voices of the dead.

Near the outskirts of this once-great metropolis, a group of survivors huddled around a makeshift fire. Their clothing was a patchwork of scavenged fabrics, their faces smeared with grime. Eyes darted nervously at every sound, every shift in the shadows. Trust was a luxury few could afford, and every stranger was a potential threat in this brutal new world.

Marauders and raiders, the predators of this new age, prowled the wasteland in gangs. They were ruthless, preying on the weak and the isolated, their humanity eroded by the struggle for survival. Armed with whatever weapons they could find or forge, they ruled through fear and violence, their reign marked by brutality and bloodshed.

Food and clean water were the most precious commodities, more valuable than gold or diamonds. The rivers and streams, once sources of life, were now toxic, poisoned by the fallout of war and industry. Water purification tablets were hoarded like treasures, and rain was a double-edged sword, bringing both the possibility of hydration and the threat of acid burns.

The survivors spoke in hushed tones of the old world, of green parks and bustling markets, of laughter and music. These memories were both a comfort and a curse, a painful reminder of all they had lost. Children, born into this hellscape, listened with wide eyes, their imaginations painting pictures of a paradise they had never known.

Beneath the ground, in the vast network of tunnels and sewers, another world existed. Those who had been driven to the depths sought refuge from the relentless sun and the marauders above. These subterranean enclaves were dark and damp, but they offered a modicum of safety. Here, the air was stale, thick with the scent of mold and human filth, but the constant threat of violence was somewhat diminished.

In the gloom, makeshift communities formed, bound together by necessity. Water was collected from trickling leaks in the walls, food scavenged from the surface or grown in small, hidden hydroponic gardens. The tunnels echoed with the murmur of voices, the shuffle of feet, and the occasional cry of a newborn, a fragile beacon of hope in the darkness.

Above ground, the landscape was punctuated by the skeletal remains of once-prosperous towns. Abandoned homes stood in silent rows, their windows like empty eyes, staring out over streets littered with debris. Shops and stores were gutted, their shelves bare, their windows shattered. Signs of life were few and far between, and when found, they were often grim.

A lone figure trudged through the desolate streets, a backpack slung over one shoulder, a makeshift spear clutched in one hand. Their movements were slow, deliberate, conserving energy, eyes scanning the surroundings for threats or opportunities. The buildings loomed like sentinels, watching, waiting.

Nature, in its relentless cycle, began to reclaim the land. Trees, twisted and stunted by radiation, pushed through the crumbling pavement. Vines crept up the sides of buildings, their green tendrils a stark contrast to the gray monotony. Animals, too, adapted to the new world, their mutations a testament to the resilience of life. Rats, larger and more aggressive, roamed the streets, and flocks of crows, their feathers iridescent with strange hues, circled the sky, scavenging the dead.

In the shadow of a collapsed overpass, a small settlement clung to existence. Tarps and sheets of metal formed crude shelters, and the smell of cooking fires mingled with the stench of unwashed bodies. Here, barter was the law, and every item had value. Ammunition, medical supplies, and clean water were the currency, and every transaction was fraught with tension.

The leader of this enclave, a woman named Mara, ruled with a mix of strength and compassion. Her face, weathered and scarred, bore witness to the trials she had endured. She moved with the confidence of someone who had survived countless battles, her eyes always scanning, always alert. Under her leadership, the settlement had managed to carve out a fragile peace, a beacon of stability in the chaos.

Yet even here, the specter of violence was never far. Rival factions coveted their resources, and the threat of raids was a constant shadow. Defenses were always manned, lookouts stationed on every high point, their eyes ever watchful. The children, too young to fight, learned quickly the art of survival, their innocence a casualty of the harsh reality.

Beyond the boundaries of this tenuous sanctuary, the land stretched out, a seemingly endless expanse of ruin. The horizon was jagged with the silhouettes of crumbled structures, and the ground was littered with the detritus of a bygone era. Rusted machinery, twisted metal, and the occasional bone told the story of a world brought to its knees.

As the sun dipped below the horizon, the sky erupted in a blaze of color, a fleeting reminder of beauty in a world so devoid of it. The temperature dropped swiftly, and the fire's warmth became a precious comfort. The night brought its own dangers, and the survivors huddled close, weapons within reach, ears straining for any sound out of the ordinary.

In this twilight world, hope was a fragile thing, but it was not yet extinguished. Among the ruins and the wreckage, life persisted, stubborn and unyielding. The human spirit, though battered and bruised, refused to surrender completely. Stories were told around the fire, tales of bravery and loss, of dreams and despair. In these moments, the survivors found a flicker of something more, a reason to continue, a reason to fight.

The wasteland was a harsh, unforgiving place, but within its desolate embrace, pockets of life endured. Each day was a struggle, each moment a test of endurance, but the spark of humanity remained. In the face of overwhelming odds, the survivors clung to that spark, nurturing it, guarding it against the encroaching darkness.

As the first stars appeared in the sky, twinkling like distant beacons, the wasteland settled into its nocturnal rhythm. The howls of mutated beasts echoed in the distance, and the wind carried the faint scent of rain. The night was long, and the road ahead was fraught with peril, but for those who survived, each dawn brought the promise of another day.

The journey through the wasteland was far from over, and the path forward remained shrouded in uncertainty. But as long as there were those willing to fight, to endure, to hope, the story of the wasteland would continue. And in that persistence, in that unwavering will to survive, there was a glimmer of something more—a testament to the indomitable spirit of humanity, even in the face of the end of the world.

CHAPTER TWO

Among the diverse enclaves, stories abounded of the Forgotten Enclave, a rumored lost haven of pre-apocalyptic knowledge and technology. Whispers of this mythical sanctuary traveled far and wide, carried by traders and wanderers. It was said to be a place where the old world's wisdom had been preserved, where scientists and engineers had sequestered themselves away, continuing their work in secret. According to legend, the Forgotten Enclave was a bastion of lost technologies, housing everything from advanced medical equipment to powerful, uncorrupted energy sources. The idea of such a place was intoxicating, offering a glimmer of hope to those who clung to the belief that humanity's former glory could one day be restored.

The exact location of the Forgotten Enclave was shrouded in mystery. Some claimed it lay deep within the irradiated forests to the northwest, while others believed it was hidden beneath the ruins of a great city, its entrance sealed and forgotten. Yet, despite the uncertainty, many set out in search of it, driven by desperation, curiosity, or the allure of the untold riches it might contain.

One such seeker was Jarek, a rugged, middle-aged man with a haunted look in his eyes. He had heard tales of the Forgotten Enclave from an old trader who had stumbled into the small settlement where Jarek had been living. The trader, a wiry, sunburnt man with a map of scars crisscrossing his face, spoke of a vault filled with wonders, guarded by an ancient, self-sustaining AI system. Jarek, who had lost everything in the cataclysm, was captivated by the idea of finding this mythical place. Perhaps there, he could find something to give his life purpose again.

Jarek's journey began in the ashes of the old world. With nothing but a tattered map and a few supplies, he ventured into the wasteland. The landscape was unforgiving, a labyrinth of twisted metal and crumbling concrete. He moved cautiously, avoiding the known territories of marauders and mutant beasts. His path took him through regions where the air was thick with radiation, where the ground glowed eerily at night, and where the very environment seemed to conspire against him.

Weeks turned into months as Jarek traversed the desolate expanse. He encountered others along the way, some fellow seekers of the Forgotten Enclave, others simply trying to survive. Some joined him for a time, forming tenuous alliances, only to part ways when their paths diverged or when the hardships proved too great. There were moments of camaraderie, fleeting glimpses of what humanity once was, but also betrayal and loss, reminders of how far they had fallen.

One night, as Jarek made camp in the ruins of an old factory, he met a woman named Elara. She was a skilled mechanic and tinkerer, with a keen mind and an even sharper wit. She had been tracking the same legends, piecing together fragments of information from various sources. She showed Jarek a device she had salvaged, a portable scanner that could detect energy signatures. It was old and temperamental, but in the right hands, it might lead them to the Enclave.

Elara and Jarek formed an uneasy partnership. They complemented each other's skills, Jarek's survival instincts and Elara's technical expertise proving invaluable. Together, they deciphered clues and navigated treacherous terrain. The scanner, though finicky, provided occasional bursts of useful data, guiding them toward areas of interest.

Their journey brought them to the edge of a vast, irradiated forest, a place whispered about in hushed tones by those who dared speak of it. The forest was dense and foreboding, the trees twisted and blackened, their branches interwoven like the bars of a cage. The air was thick with radiation, and the ground was a tangled mass of roots and undergrowth.

Jarek and Elara pressed on, the scanner guiding them deeper into the heart of the forest. The nights were filled with strange, haunting sounds, the cries of unknown creatures and the rustle of unseen movements. The air grew colder, and the trees seemed to close in around them, blocking out the light.

One evening, as they sat by their fire, Elara spoke of her past. She had been part of a small community of engineers and scientists who had survived the cataclysm by retreating into an underground bunker. They had hoped to rebuild, to salvage what they could of the old world's knowledge. But the bunker had been compromised, overrun by raiders, and Elara had barely escaped with her life. The search for the Forgotten Enclave was her way of continuing their mission, of honoring the memory of those she had lost.

Jarek listened, his own memories of loss surfacing. He spoke of his family, of the life he had once known. The weight of the past hung heavy between them, a shared burden that bound them together. In the wasteland, such connections were rare, and they drew strength from each other's resolve.

Days turned into weeks as they pushed further into the forest. The scanner led them to an old military installation, hidden beneath a canopy of trees. The entrance was buried under rubble, but with effort, they managed to clear a path. Inside, they found a labyrinth of tunnels and chambers, long abandoned and filled with debris.

The installation was a relic of a forgotten era, its walls lined with rusted equipment and faded maps. They searched room by room, piecing together fragments of the past. The deeper they went, the more signs they found of the installation's purpose. It had been a research facility, dedicated to advanced technologies and experimental projects.

In the heart of the facility, they discovered a sealed chamber. The door was heavily reinforced, but Elara's skills proved invaluable. She worked tirelessly, bypassing security systems and unlocking the mechanisms that held the door shut. When it finally opened, a hiss of stale air greeted them, and they stepped into a room bathed in the soft glow of dormant machinery.

The chamber was a treasure trove of pre-apocalyptic technology. Shelves lined with data drives, terminals still flickering with power, and in the center, a large cylindrical device that hummed with a faint, steady pulse. Elara approached it, her eyes wide with wonder. It was an energy core, unlike anything she had ever seen, a relic of the old world's pinnacle of achievement.

As they explored the chamber, they found records and blueprints, documents detailing the facility's work. The researchers had been on the verge of a breakthrough, developing technologies that could have changed the course of history. But the cataclysm had struck before they could complete their work, and the facility had been forgotten, its secrets buried in the depths of the forest.

Elara and Jarek spent days cataloging their findings, absorbing the knowledge contained within the chamber. It was a glimpse into a lost world, a beacon of hope in the darkness. The energy core, if it could be restored, had the potential to power an entire settlement, to provide clean energy and a chance for a new beginning.

But their discovery was not without danger. The activation of the chamber's systems had not gone unnoticed. As they worked, they became aware of movements outside, of figures lurking in the shadows. Marauders, drawn by the signs of life and the promise of untold riches, had found them.

Jarek and Elara fortified their position, preparing for the inevitable confrontation. The facility's defenses were still partially operational, and they used what they could to their advantage. The marauders attacked with brutal efficiency, their numbers overwhelming, but Jarek and Elara fought back with a desperation born of necessity.

The battle was fierce, the air thick with the sound of gunfire and the smell of blood. Jarek, wielding a makeshift weapon, held the line, his determination unwavering. Elara, working frantically at the control panels, managed to activate a defensive barrier, temporarily halting the marauders' advance.

In the chaos, they made a decision. The energy core, their greatest find, was too valuable to lose. Elara rigged it for transport, and with Jarek covering their escape, they fled into the tunnels. The marauders pursued them, but the labyrinthine passages worked to their advantage. They navigated the maze, using their knowledge of the facility to stay one step ahead.

Emerging from the tunnels, they found themselves back in the forest, the energy core securely in their possession. The marauders, unwilling to venture too far into the unknown, eventually gave up the chase. Jarek and Elara pressed on, their bond stronger than ever, their resolve unshaken.

Their journey was far from over, and the path ahead was fraught with peril. But they had found something precious in the heart of the wasteland, a glimmer of hope that could light the way forward. The Forgotten Enclave, once a distant dream, had become a beacon of possibility, a testament to the enduring spirit of humanity.

CHAPTER THREE

Among the myriad souls wandering the wasteland, there was a young man named Finn, whose heart was filled with stories of the Forgotten Enclave. He had grown up in the shadow of ruins, his childhood shaped by the tales of his elders who spoke of a time before the fall. They whispered of the Enclave with a mix of awe and longing, painting it as a place where humanity's lost knowledge and technology had been preserved, a beacon of hope in a world gone dark.

Finn was a dreamer, a rarity in a land where survival often left little room for dreams. His eyes, a striking blue, were filled with a determination that belied his years. He had an innate curiosity, an insatiable thirst for knowledge that set him apart from those around him. From an early age, he had devoured every story, every scrap of information about the Forgotten Enclave. It became his obsession, a beacon guiding his steps through the bleak landscape.

He had heard of Jarek and Elara's discovery, the whispers of their find spreading like wildfire among the scattered settlements. The energy core and the trove of pre-apocalyptic technology had reignited his fervor. Finn knew that finding the Enclave was his destiny, and he was prepared to face any danger, endure any hardship to reach it.

Finn's journey began in a small enclave known as the Outpost, a settlement perched precariously on the edge of a vast desert. The Outpost was a harsh place, its people hardened by the relentless sun and the scarcity of resources. Here, life was a daily struggle, and the strong preyed on the weak. Finn had learned to survive, but he had never allowed the brutality of his surroundings to extinguish his hope.

With little more than a backpack filled with basic supplies, a worn map, and a makeshift weapon, Finn set out into the desert. The map, a relic from the old world, was tattered and incomplete, but it was all he had. His journey was perilous, the sun's unforgiving heat beating down on him, the nights freezing and filled with the howls of mutated beasts. He navigated by the stars, each step taking him further into the unknown.

Weeks turned into months, and Finn's resolve was tested at every turn. He crossed desolate plains and treacherous mountains, skirted the edges of marauder territory, and scavenged what he could from the remnants of forgotten towns. Along the way, he encountered other travelers, each with their own stories and struggles. Some joined him for a time, drawn by his unyielding determination and the promise of the Forgotten Enclave.

In one such encounter, Finn met an old man named Elias. Elias was a wandering scholar, a keeper of forgotten lore, who had spent decades piecing together the fragmented history of the old world. His knowledge was vast, his mind sharp despite his advanced age. When Finn spoke of his quest for the Enclave, Elias's eyes lit up with a mix of surprise and approval. He saw in Finn a kindred spirit, someone who shared his reverence for the past and his hope for the future.

Elias decided to accompany Finn, becoming both mentor and companion. He shared his extensive knowledge, teaching Finn about the intricacies of pre-apocalyptic technology and the history of the world that had come before. Together, they deciphered old texts and maps, following clues that led them ever closer to their goal. The bond between them grew, a deep respect and friendship forming as they traveled through the wasteland.

Their journey took them to the remnants of a sprawling metropolis, its once-grand buildings now crumbling and overgrown. This city, Elias believed, held the key to locating the Forgotten Enclave. They explored its ruins, delving into underground vaults and hidden chambers, searching for any scrap of information that could guide them.

In the heart of the city, they discovered an old library, miraculously intact beneath layers of dust and decay. The shelves were filled with books and documents, a treasure trove of lost knowledge. As they combed through the library's contents, they found references to a hidden bunker, a last refuge for scientists and engineers during the cataclysm. The coordinates were cryptic, a series of numbers and symbols that Elias painstakingly deciphered.

With the location of the bunker in hand, Finn and Elias pressed on, their excitement tempered by the ever-present dangers of the wasteland. The bunker lay deep in a mountainous region, a place known for its treacherous terrain and hostile inhabitants. The journey was grueling, the mountains steep and unforgiving, the air thin and cold. But Finn's determination never wavered, and Elias's guidance kept them on the right path.

As they neared the bunker, they encountered a group of survivors, led by a woman named Lyra. Lyra was fierce and resourceful, her leadership unquestioned by those she commanded. She had heard of Finn's quest and saw in him a spark of hope, a chance to change the fate of her people. She offered her assistance, her group providing much-needed strength and numbers.

Together, they reached the entrance to the bunker, hidden behind a waterfall in a secluded valley. The entrance was sealed, but Elara's technical skills, which Finn had learned of from other wanderers, had given them the means to bypass such obstacles. Using Elias's knowledge and Finn's determination, they worked tirelessly to open the door.

When the door finally creaked open, a rush of cold, stale air greeted them. They stepped into the darkness, their flashlights cutting through the gloom. The bunker was a labyrinth of corridors and chambers, filled with the remnants of the old world. They moved cautiously, aware that the bunker's automated defenses might still be active.

Deep within the bunker, they found a control room, its walls lined with monitors and control panels. Elias, his eyes alight with excitement, began to activate the systems, bringing the bunker to life. The monitors flickered on, revealing a treasure trove of data and technology. The Forgotten Enclave was real, and they had found it.

As they explored the bunker, they discovered a central chamber, housing the core of the Enclave's technology. It was a massive, humming machine, surrounded by banks of computers and storage devices. Elias worked feverishly, accessing the data, while Finn and Lyra secured the perimeter.

The data they uncovered was astounding. It included blueprints for advanced energy sources, medical technologies, and even plans for rebuilding society. The knowledge contained within the bunker had the potential to change everything, to bring about a new era of hope and progress.

In the dimly lit control room of the Forgotten Enclave, the air was thick with a mixture of excitement and tension. Monitors flickered to life, casting an eerie glow over the faces of Finn, Elias, Lyra, and their small group of survivors. The hum of machinery, dormant for decades, now thrummed with renewed energy.

Finn stood by a large terminal, his eyes wide with wonder as he took in the array of data scrolling across the screens. "I can't believe it," he murmured, more to himself than anyone else. "It's real. We actually found it."

Elias, his hands deftly working the controls, glanced over at Finn, a proud smile on his weathered face. "I've spent my entire life chasing fragments of the past, but I never truly believed we'd find something like this," he said, his voice tinged with awe. "This technology... it could change everything."

Lyra, ever practical, leaned against a console, her arms crossed. "We need to focus on securing this place. The signal we activated won't go unnoticed for long. Marauders will be on us like vultures," she said, her tone firm.

Finn nodded, his excitement tempered by the reality of their situation. "You're right, Lyra. We need to make sure we can hold this place, at least long enough to gather what we can and get out."

Elara, a skilled mechanic and the group's tech expert, stepped forward, holding a portable storage device. "I've managed to download a substantial amount of data already," she said. "Blueprints, medical research, energy production methods. It's incredible. But there's so much more here. We need time."

Elias's eyes lit up as he glanced at the storage device. "We need to prioritize the most critical information. Energy production and medical advancements first," he suggested. "Those could make the most immediate impact on our survival."

Lyra pushed off the console and moved closer to the group. "We've fortified the entrance as best we can, but it's only a matter of time before we're discovered," she said. "We'll set up shifts. Some of us will continue to download data, while others stand guard. We can't afford to lose any of this."

Finn looked around at his companions, his resolve strengthening. "This is our chance," he said. "We can bring back the knowledge we've lost, rebuild our world. But we have to be smart about it. We can't let greed or fear drive us apart."

Elara nodded, her expression determined. "We should also document everything we find here," she said. "Create backups, spread the knowledge as far and wide as we can. Even if we don't make it, someone else might."

The group fell silent for a moment, the weight of their discovery settling over them. They were standing at the precipice of a new era, but the path ahead was fraught with danger.

Lyra broke the silence, her voice low but resolute. "We have to protect this place and each other," she said. "We came here together, and we'll leave together."

Elias placed a hand on Finn's shoulder, his eyes filled with a mixture of pride and hope. "You've done well, Finn," he said. "You've brought us here, and now it's up to us to see this through. This is just the beginning."

Finn smiled, feeling a sense of purpose he had never known before. "We won't let this knowledge be lost again," he vowed. "We'll make sure the world remembers."

As the group set to work, the control room buzzed with activity. They were a small team, but their determination was unyielding. The Forgotten Enclave had been found, and with it, a new hope for the future. But the challenges ahead were immense, and the wasteland was not kind to dreamers.

CHAPTER FOUR

As the group delved deeper into the bunker, the extent of their discovery became apparent. The Forgotten Enclave was not just a cache of old technologies; it was a fully operational facility, miraculously preserved through the cataclysm and the years of desolation that followed. Advanced machinery hummed softly in the background, and the walls were lined with screens displaying streams of data.

Finn led the way, his heart pounding with a mix of excitement and trepidation. The air was cool and sterile, a stark contrast to the harsh, polluted environment outside. He marveled at the pristine condition of the equipment, each piece a testament to the ingenuity of the pre-apocalyptic world.

In the central chamber, Finn and his companions came across a large, reinforced door. Unlike the other doors they had encountered, this one was sealed tight, with an electronic panel beside it. Elara examined the panel, her fingers flying over the touch screen as she worked to bypass the security protocols.

"This is it," she said, her voice tinged with anticipation. "Whatever's behind this door, it's important."

With a final tap, the panel beeped, and the door slowly slid open, revealing a vast room filled with rows of servers and data banks. In the center of the room stood a tall, sleek console, its surface glowing with a soft blue light.

As they approached the console, it activated, and a holographic image flickered to life above it. The figure was humanoid but ethereal, composed of shimmering light. It regarded them with a gaze that seemed almost sentient.

"Welcome, travelers," the figure intoned, its voice smooth and resonant. "I am Oracle, the artificial intelligence tasked with preserving and protecting the knowledge of the Forgotten Enclave."

Finn's eyes widened in awe. "Oracle," he repeated, stepping closer. "You were designed to protect this place?"

"Indeed," Oracle replied. "I was created to ensure that the knowledge and technologies developed here would survive, even if the world outside did not. My primary directive is to safeguard this information and assist those who seek to rebuild."

Elias stepped forward, his scholarly curiosity piqued. "Oracle, we are here to learn, to reclaim the knowledge lost in the cataclysm. Can you help us?"

Oracle's holographic form shimmered slightly as it processed the request. "I can provide access to the vast library of data stored within this facility. However, this knowledge is powerful and must be used responsibly. Tell me, what do you seek to achieve with this information?"

Finn exchanged a glance with his companions before speaking. "We want to rebuild," he said earnestly. "Our world is broken, and people are suffering. We believe that with the knowledge contained here, we can make things better. We can restore some of what was lost."

Oracle regarded them for a moment, its expression unreadable. "Very well," it said finally. "I will grant you access to the library. But be warned: the path to rebuilding is fraught with challenges, and the misuse of this knowledge could lead to further destruction."

Elara stepped forward, her eyes fixed on the holographic figure. "We understand the risks," she said. "But we also understand the potential. We will use this knowledge wisely."

Oracle nodded, and the console lit up with a series of holographic displays. "Begin your studies," it said. "I will assist you in navigating the archives and accessing the information you need."

The group set to work, each member diving into the vast repository of data. Finn and Elara focused on energy production and medical technologies, while Elias delved into historical records and blueprints. Lyra and her team fortified their position, ensuring that they could defend the Enclave against any threats.

As they worked, Finn felt a sense of purpose and hope he had never known before. The knowledge contained within the Enclave was astounding. They found detailed schematics for advanced energy reactors, methods for purifying water, and medical treatments that could eradicate diseases that had plagued the wasteland for years.

One evening, as Finn pored over a particularly complex set of blueprints, Oracle materialized beside him. "You have a keen mind," the AI said. "Your understanding of this technology is impressive."

Finn looked up, a hint of a smile on his lips. "I've always been fascinated by the old world," he admitted. "It's incredible to finally see it up close, to understand how things used to work."

Oracle's gaze softened, if such a thing were possible for an artificial intelligence. "The world that was is gone," it said. "But the knowledge and the spirit of innovation that created it live on. Use them wisely, and you may yet build a better future."

Days turned into weeks as the group absorbed as much information as they could. The Enclave became a hub of activity, a place of learning and planning. They set goals, mapped out strategies, and began to envision a world rebuilt with the knowledge they had gained.

But the wasteland was never far away, and the threat of discovery loomed large. One afternoon, as Lyra was scouting the perimeter, she spotted movement in the distance. She hurried back to the Enclave, her expression grim.

"We've got company," she announced. "Looks like a raiding party, heavily armed."

Finn's heart sank. "How long do we have?"

"Not long," Lyra replied. "We need to prepare."

The group mobilized, setting traps and fortifying their defenses. Finn and Elara worked frantically to secure the most critical data, ensuring that even if they were forced to flee, the knowledge they had gained would not be lost.

As the raiders closed in, Oracle activated the Enclave's internal defenses. Automated turrets and barriers sprang to life, creating a formidable line of defense. The battle that ensued was fierce, the air filled with the sounds of gunfire and explosions.

Finn fought alongside his companions, his heart pounding with fear and determination. The raiders were relentless, but the Enclave's defenses held strong. As the sun dipped below the horizon, the last of the raiders were driven back, retreating into the darkness.

Breathless and exhausted, the group regrouped in the control room. "We did it," Finn said, his voice filled with a mixture of relief and disbelief. "We held them off."

Lyra nodded, wiping sweat from her brow. "For now," she said. "But we can't stay here forever. Sooner or later, they'll come back with reinforcements."

Elias, who had been studying the maps and data, looked up with a thoughtful expression. "We need to take this knowledge back to our people," he said. "Share it, spread it. Only then can we hope to rebuild."

Oracle materialized beside them, its presence a comforting constant. "The Enclave's knowledge is now yours," it said. "But remember, knowledge alone is not enough. It is how you use it that will determine the future."

Finn nodded, feeling the weight of responsibility settle on his shoulders. "We'll make sure it's used wisely," he vowed. "We'll rebuild our world, one step at a time."

As they prepared to leave, Finn took one last look at the Enclave, the place that had given him hope and purpose. The journey ahead was uncertain, but for the first time, he felt truly ready to face it. The knowledge and technology of the Forgotten Enclave would be their guiding light, a beacon in the darkness.

And with that, they set out into the wasteland once more, determined to build a better future from the ashes of the past.

As Finn and his companions prepared to leave the Forgotten Enclave, Oracle materialized once more, its holographic form standing tall in the center of the control room. The AI's presence filled the space with a sense of gravitas, a reminder of the weight of the knowledge they had uncovered.

"Before you go," Oracle began, "there is something you must understand about the Enclave and the intentions of its creators."

Finn paused, turning to face Oracle fully. "What do you mean?"

Oracle's form flickered slightly, as if contemplating how best to convey the information. "The Enclave was established by a coalition of scientists, engineers, and visionaries who foresaw the impending cataclysm. They understood that the knowledge and technologies they had developed could not be allowed to perish, even if civilization fell. Their intention was to create a sanctuary, a repository of human achievement, to safeguard humanity's legacy and ensure that future generations could rebuild."

Elias stepped closer, his eyes alight with curiosity. "So this place was designed to be found? To be a beacon of hope for those who survived?"

"Precisely," Oracle confirmed. "The creators of the Enclave believed that the knowledge contained here could serve as the foundation for a new beginning. They implemented advanced security measures to protect it, but also designed the Enclave to respond to those who demonstrated a genuine desire to use its knowledge for the greater good."

Elara nodded thoughtfully. "That explains the sophisticated defenses and the challenges we faced getting in. But what about the dangers? Surely they knew that such powerful technology could be misused."

Oracle's gaze shifted to her, its expression serious. "The creators were acutely aware of the potential for misuse. They encoded ethical guidelines and fail-safes into the Enclave's systems, but ultimately, the responsibility rests with those who access this knowledge. Power, in any form, can corrupt. It is imperative that you and those you share this with remain vigilant and use this knowledge wisely."

Finn absorbed Oracle's words, the weight of the responsibility settling heavily on his shoulders. "We will," he said firmly. "But we need to understand what we're dealing with. What are the most important technologies here that could help us rebuild?"

Oracle nodded, its holographic form shifting to display a series of images and diagrams. "There are several key technologies that can aid in the reconstruction of society:

1. **Energy Production:** The Enclave houses blueprints for advanced energy reactors, capable of generating clean, renewable power. These reactors can provide electricity to entire settlements, fueling industry, communication, and daily life.

2. **Water Purification:** The technology to purify contaminated water sources is crucial. The Enclave's systems include methods to remove toxins and pollutants, making water safe for consumption and irrigation.

3. **Medical Advances:** From advanced surgical techniques to vaccines and treatments for diseases, the medical knowledge stored here can save countless lives. This includes methods for combating the radiation poisoning that plagues much of the wasteland.

4. **Agricultural Innovations:** The Enclave contains data on sustainable farming practices and genetically modified crops that can thrive in harsh conditions, ensuring a stable food supply.

5. **Communication Systems:** Restoring long-distance communication networks will allow for coordination between distant communities, fostering cooperation and mutual support.

"These technologies, if used wisely, can lay the groundwork for a new era of prosperity. However, the misuse of such power could lead to further devastation. It is essential to establish a framework of governance and ethical oversight to guide the use of these resources."

Lyra, ever pragmatic, voiced the concern that was on everyone's mind. "What's to stop the wrong people from taking this knowledge and using it for their own gain? We've seen what power can do in the wrong hands."

Oracle's form shimmered, a somber note in its voice. "That is a risk that cannot be entirely mitigated. However, by spreading the knowledge widely and ensuring that it is not concentrated in the hands of a few, you can create a system of checks and balances. Encourage collaboration, transparency, and accountability. Foster a culture that values the well-being of the community over individual gain."

Elias nodded in agreement. "It's up to us to set the right example, to build a foundation of trust and cooperation. We have a chance to do things differently, to learn from the mistakes of the past."

Finn looked around at his companions, seeing the determination and resolve mirrored in their faces. "We have a long road ahead," he said. "But we have the tools and the knowledge to make a real difference. We can rebuild, not just physically, but socially and ethically. We can create a world that's better than the one we lost."

As they made their final preparations to leave the Enclave, Oracle imparted one last piece of wisdom. "Remember, the true strength of humanity lies not in its technology, but in its spirit. The will to survive, to adapt, to overcome adversity—that is your greatest asset. Use the knowledge you have gained here to build a future worthy of that spirit."

With that, the group set out once more into the wasteland, the precious data carefully secured and their hearts filled with a renewed sense of purpose. They knew the journey ahead would be fraught with challenges, but they also knew that they carried with them the hope and the means to rebuild a world from the ashes.

As they trekked back towards their settlement, Finn couldn't help but feel a surge of optimism. The vision of a thriving, restored society guided his steps. The wasteland was still a harsh and dangerous place, but within its desolation, the seeds of a new beginning had been planted. The Forgotten Enclave had given them the tools they needed, and now it was up to them to shape the future.

CHAPTER FIVE

As Finn and his companions made their way back to their new settlement, the weight of their discovery hung heavy on their minds. They knew they carried the seeds of a new beginning, but they also understood the immense responsibility that came with it. However, their return was not as discreet as they had hoped. Unbeknownst to them, news of their find had leaked to a nearby enclave, one ruled by a ruthless warlord named Kade.

Kade's enclave was known for its harsh conditions and even harsher leadership. The warlord maintained power through fear and brute force, his raiders enforcing his rule with an iron fist. When word reached Kade of the Forgotten Enclave and its treasures, he saw an opportunity to cement his dominion over the region. The thought of possessing advanced technology and abundant resources was too tempting to resist. He quickly mobilized a band of his most loyal and vicious raiders, intent on seizing the Enclave for himself.

Finn and his group, unaware of the impending threat, continued their journey, focused on securing and disseminating the knowledge they had gained. It wasn't until they were within sight of their settlement that they noticed the first signs of trouble. Smoke rose in the distance, and the sound of gunfire echoed across the barren landscape.

Lyra, always vigilant, raised her binoculars and surveyed the scene. "Raiders," she muttered, her face grim. "And they're attacking our settlement."

Finn's heart pounded in his chest. "We need to get there, now!" he urged, breaking into a run. The others followed, their determination renewed by the urgency of the situation.

As they approached the outskirts of their settlement, the full extent of the chaos became clear. Buildings were ablaze, and the settlers, outnumbered and outgunned, fought desperately to defend their homes. Finn's group quickly joined the fray, their presence bolstering the defenders' morale.

Lyra took command, her tactical mind quickly assessing the situation. "We need to secure the perimeter and push them back," she shouted. "Elara, Elias, find high ground and provide cover. Finn, with me!"

The battle was fierce and chaotic. Finn fought with a ferocity he hadn't known he possessed, driven by the need to protect his people and the knowledge they had risked so much to obtain. The raiders were ruthless, but the defenders fought with the desperation of those who had nothing left to lose.

In the midst of the fighting, Finn spotted Kade, the warlord directing his men with cold efficiency. Their eyes met across the battlefield, and in that moment, Finn knew that this man would stop at nothing to seize the Enclave's secrets.

With a surge of determination, Finn fought his way through the melee, his path set on reaching Kade. The two clashed in a brutal confrontation, their weapons ringing out in the chaos. Kade was a formidable opponent, his strength and skill honed by years of violence.

"You can't win," Kade sneered, his voice dripping with contempt. "I will take the Enclave and all its treasures. You're nothing but a boy playing at hero."

Finn gritted his teeth, blocking a powerful strike. "You're wrong," he retorted. "The Enclave isn't just a treasure to be plundered. It's hope. And I won't let you destroy that."

Their battle raged on, but even as Finn fought, a moral dilemma gnawed at him. He had sworn to use the Enclave's knowledge for the greater good, to rebuild and not destroy. Yet here he was, caught in a violent struggle that seemed to betray that very vow. Was he becoming what he despised? Was he any different from the marauders, fighting for control and power?

The fight with Kade reached a critical point. Finn, driven by sheer willpower, managed to disarm the warlord, his weapon clattering to the ground. He held his makeshift blade to Kade's throat, the warlord's life in his hands.

"Do it," Kade spat, his eyes filled with defiance. "Kill me and take your place as the new warlord. It's what you want, isn't it?"

Finn hesitated, the weight of his decisions pressing down on him. He glanced around at the destruction, at the faces of his friends and fellow settlers, all looking to him for guidance. The path he chose now would define the future.

"No," Finn said, lowering his weapon. "I'm not like you. This isn't about power or control. It's about building a better world."

He stepped back, signaling his companions to bind Kade. "We're taking you prisoner," he said firmly. "You'll answer for your crimes, but we won't become what we're fighting against."

The battle gradually subsided as the remaining raiders, seeing their leader captured, either surrendered or fled. The defenders, battered and exhausted, began the arduous task of tending to the wounded and extinguishing the fires.

As dawn broke over the settlement, Finn and his companions gathered in the central square. The relief of victory was tempered by the heavy losses they had suffered. Yet amidst the destruction, there was a renewed sense of hope and purpose.

Elias approached Finn, placing a hand on his shoulder. "You did the right thing," he said. "It would have been easy to give in to anger and hatred, but you chose a different path. That's what makes you a true leader."

Finn nodded, his resolve strengthened. "We have a lot of work to do," he said. "But we have the knowledge and the means to start rebuilding. And we'll do it together."

Lyra stepped forward, her expression determined. "We need to fortify our defenses and make sure the Enclave's secrets are protected. But more than that, we need to start spreading this knowledge, forming alliances with other settlements. We can't do this alone."

Elara and the others voiced their agreement, and plans were quickly set into motion. The Enclave's data was carefully backed up and distributed among trusted allies. Training sessions were organized to teach settlers how to use and maintain the advanced technologies.

As the settlement began to rebuild, Finn felt a renewed sense of purpose. The journey had been long and fraught with challenges, but they had emerged stronger and more united. The knowledge of the Forgotten Enclave was a powerful tool, but it was the spirit and determination of the people that would truly rebuild their world.

And so, under Finn's leadership, the settlement began to thrive. They formed alliances with neighboring enclaves, sharing knowledge and resources, fostering a new era of cooperation and mutual support. The path ahead was still uncertain, but for the first time in a long while, the future seemed bright.

CHAPTER SIX

As the dust settled and the survivors began to regroup, Finn knew they needed to secure the Forgotten Enclave's defenses if they were to fend off any future attacks. The raid had been a wake-up call; the knowledge and technology they had uncovered were powerful, but also a tempting target for those who sought to exploit them.

With Kade securely imprisoned and under guard, Finn gathered his closest allies in the central chamber of the Enclave. The group included Lyra, Elias, Elara, and a few other key figures from their settlement. They stood around the glowing console where Oracle's holographic form flickered to life once more.

"Oracle," Finn began, "we need to understand the full extent of the Enclave's defenses. We were able to hold off the raiders this time, but we need to be better prepared for future attacks."

Oracle's form shimmered, the AI's presence calming yet authoritative. "The Enclave's defenses are extensive and designed to protect its contents from external threats. I can provide access to automated turrets, energy shields, and surveillance systems. However, it is crucial that these defenses are used judiciously to prevent them from becoming instruments of oppression."

Elara stepped forward, her eyes bright with determination. "We need to integrate these systems with our settlement's existing defenses. If we can create a cohesive security network, we can protect not just the Enclave, but our people as well."

Finn nodded. "Let's do it. Oracle, show us how to activate and control the defenses."

The next few days were a blur of activity. Elara and Elias worked tirelessly to understand the Enclave's advanced technology, guided by Oracle's instructions. They installed automated turrets at key points around the settlement, connected to a central control system that could be monitored from the Enclave's command center. Energy shields were deployed, creating invisible barriers that could repel attackers while allowing friendly forces to move freely.

Finn, meanwhile, focused on fortifying the perimeter and training the settlers to use the new defenses effectively. He knew that technology alone wouldn't be enough; they needed to be prepared, vigilant, and united.

One evening, as Finn and Lyra were making rounds to inspect the newly installed systems, a distant rumble caught their attention. Lyra raised her binoculars and scanned the horizon. "We've got movement," she said, her voice tense. "Looks like another raiding party. Bigger this time."

Finn's heart raced. "How much time do we have?"

"Not much," Lyra replied. "Maybe an hour, if we're lucky."

Finn turned to the nearest sentry. "Sound the alarm. Everyone, to your positions!"

The settlement sprang into action, the air filled with the sounds of people rushing to prepare. The automated turrets whirred to life, their sensors tracking the approaching raiders. Energy shields shimmered into existence, casting a faint glow over the perimeter.

Finn and Lyra took their positions in the command center, where they could monitor the battle and direct the defenses. Elara and Elias were there as well, ready to manage the technical aspects of the systems.

The raiders appeared on the horizon, a dark, menacing swarm. Kade had not given up easily, and it seemed he had rallied more forces for a second assault. They approached with a brutal efficiency, their weapons glinting in the fading light.

"Here they come," Lyra muttered, her eyes fixed on the monitors.

The first wave of raiders hit the energy shields, which held firm against the onslaught. The automated turrets began to fire, their precision targeting picking off attackers with deadly accuracy. The battle was intense, the air filled with the sounds of gunfire and explosions.

Finn watched the scene unfold on the screens, his hands clenched into fists. "We need to hold them off long enough for our people to regroup and counterattack," he said. "Elara, can you increase the power to the shields?"

Elara nodded, her fingers flying over the control panel. "I'm on it. Just keep them busy."

As the shields intensified, the raiders' progress slowed, their ranks thinning under the relentless barrage from the turrets. But Finn knew it wouldn't be enough to just hold them off; they needed to push them back.

"Lyra, take a team and hit them from the flank," Finn ordered. "Elias, coordinate with the other squads and launch a counterattack from the north. I'll direct the defenses from here."

Lyra nodded, already moving to gather her team. Elias gave a quick salute and headed out to relay the orders. Finn took a deep breath, focusing on the task at hand. He knew the Enclave's defenses were powerful, but they needed to be used strategically to avoid unnecessary casualties.

The plan unfolded with precision. Lyra's team hit the raiders from the side, catching them off guard and causing chaos in their ranks. Elias led a coordinated strike from the north, driving the attackers back toward the energy shields. The automated turrets continued their deadly work, cutting down any who ventured too close.

As the raiders faltered, Finn saw an opportunity. "Elara, activate the sonic disruptors," he said, his voice steady despite the tension.

Elara hesitated for a moment, then nodded. "Activating now."

A low, pulsing hum filled the air as the disruptors came online. The raiders clutched their heads, disoriented by the intense sound waves. It was the opening Finn had been waiting for.

"All units, advance!" he shouted into the comms.

The settlers surged forward, pressing the advantage. The raiders, demoralized and overwhelmed, began to retreat. Finn watched as they fled into the distance, a sense of relief washing over him. They had defended their home, and more importantly, they had done so without resorting to the same brutality that characterized their enemies.

As the last of the raiders disappeared from view, Finn slumped back in his chair, exhausted but triumphant. The settlement had held, and the Enclave's secrets were safe—for now.

Elara turned to him, a tired but satisfied smile on her face. "We did it, Finn. We actually did it."

Finn nodded, feeling a profound sense of accomplishment. "Yes, but we need to stay vigilant. Kade won't give up that easily. We have to be ready for anything."

Lyra re-entered the command center, her face smeared with dirt and sweat, but her eyes shining with determination. "The raiders are in full retreat," she reported. "Our people fought bravely. We've secured the perimeter, but we should expect more attacks."

Elias joined them, his expression thoughtful. "We need to be careful with this technology, Finn. It's powerful, and we've seen today how easily it could be used for destruction. We have to ensure it remains a tool for rebuilding, not for warfare."

Finn nodded, understanding the gravity of Elias's words. "You're right. We have a responsibility to use this knowledge wisely. We'll need to establish guidelines and ensure that everyone understands the importance of ethical use."

Oracle's holographic form flickered to life once more. "You have proven your ingenuity and bravery, Finn. But remember, the true challenge lies not in defending this place, but in building a future that honors the principles upon which the Enclave was founded."

Finn looked around at his companions, feeling a deep sense of camaraderie and shared purpose. "We will," he vowed. "We'll use this knowledge to rebuild, to create a better world. And we'll do it together."

The days that followed were filled with rebuilding and fortifying. The settlers worked tirelessly to repair the damage from the attack, using the Enclave's technology to strengthen their defenses and improve their living conditions. Training sessions were held to teach everyone how to operate and maintain the advanced systems, ensuring that the knowledge was widely shared and understood.

Finn and his team also focused on establishing a council to oversee the ethical use of the Enclave's resources. Representatives from various settlements were invited to join, fostering a spirit of cooperation and mutual support. They drafted guidelines and protocols, emphasizing the importance of transparency, accountability, and the collective good.

The threat of future attacks remained, but the settlement was stronger and more united than ever. They had faced their first major test and emerged victorious, not just through strength of arms, but through their commitment to a higher purpose.

One evening, as Finn stood on a hill overlooking the settlement, Oracle appeared beside him. The AI's presence was a comforting reminder of the legacy they were now part of.

"You have done well, Finn," Oracle said. "But the journey is far from over. There will be many challenges ahead, and the choices you make will shape the future."

Finn nodded, feeling the weight of responsibility but also the strength of his resolve. "I know. But we're ready. We'll face whatever comes, and we'll do it together."

As the sun set over the horizon, casting a warm glow over the settlement, Finn felt a deep sense of hope. The Forgotten Enclave had given them the tools to rebuild, but it was their spirit, their determination, and their unity that would truly shape the future.

And with that, Finn turned back to his people, ready to lead them into a new dawn.

CHAPTER SEVEN

As the settlement began to stabilize and rebuild, Oracle called for a meeting with Finn and the key leaders of the community. The holographic AI appeared in the center of the room, its presence commanding everyone's attention.

"Finn," Oracle began, "I have observed your efforts and your commitment to using the knowledge of the Enclave responsibly. However, the dangers of concentrating this power in one place are significant. To ensure the knowledge is used ethically and effectively, I propose a compromise."

Finn leaned forward, his interest piqued. "What kind of compromise?"

Oracle's holographic form shifted, displaying a map of the surrounding region with several enclaves marked. "We must carefully select trustworthy leaders from various enclaves to share the knowledge responsibly. This council of leaders will oversee the dissemination and application of the Enclave's technology, ensuring it benefits all and is not misused."

Elias nodded thoughtfully. "That makes sense. By spreading the knowledge and involving multiple communities, we can create a system of checks and balances. It reduces the risk of any one group gaining too much power."

Elara added, "It also fosters cooperation and mutual support. Each enclave can contribute its strengths, and we can all learn from each other."

Finn considered the proposal carefully. He knew the risks of revealing the Enclave's secrets, but he also understood the potential benefits. The thought of uniting the scattered enclaves and working together towards a common goal was compelling.

"I believe this is the best path forward," Finn said finally. "We need to balance the risks and benefits, and this compromise offers a way to do that. We'll reach out to the other enclaves and propose forming a council to oversee the use of the Enclave's knowledge."

Lyra stepped forward, her eyes filled with determination. "I'll organize a team to make contact with the neighboring enclaves. We'll need to identify leaders who share our vision and are committed to the greater good."

With the plan in motion, the settlement prepared to reach out to the surrounding enclaves. Finn and his companions drafted messages explaining their discovery and proposing a meeting to discuss the formation of a council. They emphasized the importance of unity and the potential benefits of sharing the Enclave's knowledge.

Teams were dispatched to the various enclaves, each led by trusted members of Finn's group. Lyra led a team to the Green Haven, while Elias and Elara traveled to the Technocrat's Enclave. Other teams were sent to the Freehold and smaller settlements scattered across the wasteland.

The responses were mixed. Some enclaves were wary, suspicious of Finn's motives and the promise of advanced technology. Others were intrigued, seeing the potential for rebuilding and improving their lives. Slowly, the leaders of the most influential enclaves agreed to meet.

The gathering took place in a neutral location, a large, abandoned building that had once been a community center.

The leaders of each enclave arrived with their entourages, their expressions a mix of curiosity, skepticism, and hope.

Finn stood at the center of the room, flanked by Lyra, Elias, and Elara. He took a deep breath and addressed the assembled leaders.

"Thank you all for coming," he began. "We stand at a crossroads. The knowledge and technology we have uncovered in the Forgotten Enclave have the potential to rebuild our world, to create a future better than the one we lost. But with this power comes great responsibility. We cannot afford to let it fall into the wrong hands or be used for selfish purposes."

He paused, letting his words sink in. "That's why we propose forming a council, made up of representatives from each of our enclaves. This council will oversee the dissemination and application of the Enclave's knowledge, ensuring it benefits everyone and is used ethically."

The room was silent for a moment before one of the leaders, an elderly woman from the Green Haven, spoke up. "How can we trust that this council will act in everyone's best interest? We've seen too many examples of power corrupting those who wield it."

Elias stepped forward. "By spreading the knowledge and involving multiple communities, we create a system of checks and balances. Each enclave will have a voice, and decisions will be made collectively. Transparency and accountability will be our guiding principles."

Another leader, a stern-faced man from the Technocrat's Enclave, nodded thoughtfully. "And what about the technology itself? How do we ensure it is not misused?"

Elara addressed his concern. "We propose implementing strict guidelines and protocols for the use of the Enclave's technology. These will be overseen by the council, and any violations will be dealt with swiftly. The goal is to use this knowledge to improve lives, not to create new forms of oppression."

The discussion continued for hours, with each leader voicing their concerns and questions. Finn and his team answered as best they could, emphasizing the importance of unity and cooperation. Slowly, the initial skepticism began to give way to a cautious optimism.

In the end, the leaders agreed to form the council, each pledging to work together for the common good. The first meeting of the newly formed Council of Enclaves was scheduled, and representatives were chosen to begin drafting the guidelines and protocols for the use of the Enclave's knowledge.

As the meeting concluded, Finn felt a sense of relief and hope. They had taken the first step towards a new era of cooperation and rebuilding. The challenges ahead were immense, but for the first time, they had a chance to shape their own future.

Oracle appeared beside Finn as the leaders began to depart, its presence a silent testament to their achievement.

"You have done well, Finn," Oracle said. "The path you have chosen is not the easiest, but it is the one that holds the most promise for a better future."

Finn nodded, feeling the weight of responsibility but also the strength of their collective resolve. "We have a long way to go," he said. "But we're ready to face whatever comes. Together."

As the sun set over the wasteland, casting a golden glow over the settlement, Finn looked out over the horizon with a renewed sense of purpose. The journey had been long and fraught with challenges, but they had found a way forward. The knowledge of the Forgotten Enclave was a powerful tool, but it was their unity, their spirit, and their determination that would truly rebuild their world.

And with that, Finn turned to join his companions, ready to lead them into the future they were creating together.

CHAPTER EIGHT

The days that followed were a whirlwind of activity and diplomacy for Finn and his team. Reaching out to the leaders of several enclaves required careful planning and strategic thinking. They had to choose their allies wisely, seeking those who had shown not only wisdom but also a genuine desire for peace and collaboration.

Finn, Lyra, Elias, and Elara began their journey by visiting the Green Haven, a lush valley enclave known for its cooperative governance and sustainable practices. The leader, Elder Mira, was an elderly woman whose sharp mind and compassionate heart had earned her the respect of her people. Finn hoped she would see the potential in the Forgotten Enclave's knowledge.

As they approached the entrance to Green Haven, they were met by a group of wary guards. Lyra stepped forward, explaining their purpose and requesting an audience with Elder Mira. After a tense few moments, the guards led them through the valley, where they marveled at the thriving crops and well-maintained community.

Elder Mira greeted them in a large, sunlit hall, her piercing eyes studying each of them carefully. "Welcome," she said, her voice calm but commanding. "I've heard of your discovery. Tell me why I should trust you and your intentions."

Finn took a deep breath and began to explain. "Elder Mira, we have found a repository of advanced knowledge and technology, created by those who foresaw the cataclysm. This knowledge has the potential to help us rebuild, to create a better future for all of us. But we can't do it alone. We need the wisdom and cooperation of leaders like you to ensure it's used responsibly."

Mira's eyes narrowed. "Knowledge is power, and power can corrupt. How do we know you won't become another warlord, using this technology to dominate others?"

Elias stepped forward, his voice steady. "That's why we propose forming a council, with representatives from each enclave. This council will oversee the use of the Enclave's knowledge, ensuring transparency and accountability. We're here to work with you, not to impose our will."

Elara added, "We've already set up protocols and guidelines for the ethical use of this technology. We believe that by sharing this knowledge and involving multiple communities, we can prevent any one group from abusing it."

Elder Mira listened carefully, her expression thoughtful. "Actions speak louder than words," she said finally. "Show me this technology. Prove to me that it can bring positive change."

Finn nodded, ready for this challenge. "We have brought a portable water purifier from the Enclave. It can turn even the most contaminated water into clean, drinkable water. Let us demonstrate."

They led Elder Mira and a group of her advisors to a nearby stream, where they set up the purifier. The stream, polluted and murky, was an ideal test. As the purifier hummed to life, it began to filter the water, removing toxins and impurities. Within minutes, clear water flowed from the device.

Finn handed a cup of the purified water to Elder Mira. She examined it closely, then took a cautious sip. Her eyes widened in surprise and approval. "This is remarkable," she said. "Such technology could save lives and improve the quality of life for many."

Seeing her reaction, Finn pressed on. "This is just one example of what we can achieve together. Imagine what we could do with advanced energy sources, medical technologies, and sustainable agriculture. But we need your help, your wisdom, to guide us."

Elder Mira nodded slowly. "I see the potential. Very well, I will join your council and support your efforts, provided we maintain a clear focus on ethical use and transparency."

With Elder Mira's support secured, Finn and his team moved on to the next enclave, the Technocrat's Enclave. This enclave was known for its rigid hierarchy and advanced technology, but also for its isolationist policies. Convincing its leader, Administrator Voss, would be a significant challenge.

The Technocrat's Enclave was a stark contrast to Green Haven, with sleek, metallic buildings and an air of efficiency. As they were escorted through the enclave, Finn noticed the advanced machinery and technology in use, a testament to the enclave's capabilities.

Administrator Voss received them in a sterile, high-tech office, his demeanor cold and analytical. "You have come to share your discovery," he said, his tone flat. "Explain why we should join you."

Finn took a different approach, knowing Voss valued logic and pragmatism. "Administrator Voss, the knowledge we've uncovered includes advanced energy production, medical treatments, and agricultural innovations. Your enclave already excels in these areas, but imagine the possibilities if we combined our resources and expertise. We can achieve more together than we ever could alone."

Voss's expression remained impassive. "And what do you expect in return? What assurances do we have that this council you propose will not be a burden or a threat to our autonomy?"

Elara stepped in, her technical expertise lending credibility to their proposal. "We envision a collaborative effort where each enclave retains its autonomy but benefits from shared knowledge and resources. The council will function as a mediator and facilitator, ensuring that the technology is used ethically and effectively."

Voss leaned back in his chair, considering their words. "Show me proof of your capabilities."

Finn nodded. "We have brought blueprints for an advanced energy reactor. This reactor can provide clean, renewable energy far more efficiently than current methods. Allow us to present it to your engineers."

The presentation took place in a large, well-equipped laboratory. Elara and Elias explained the reactor's design, its safety features, and its potential applications. The Technocrat's engineers were skeptical at first but gradually warmed to the idea as they saw the detailed plans and understood the reactor's benefits.

After the presentation, Administrator Voss seemed more open. "Your proposal has merit. I will join your council, but I will also expect strict adherence to the principles of efficiency and mutual benefit."

With the support of the Technocrat's Enclave secured, Finn and his team continued their mission, reaching out to the Freehold and other smaller settlements. Each meeting presented its own challenges, but Finn's sincerity, the practical demonstrations of the Enclave's technology, and the promise of a cooperative future gradually won over the skeptical leaders.

The Freehold was particularly challenging, with its anarchic structure and fierce independence. Its leader, a charismatic woman named Zara, was initially resistant to the idea of any form of centralized authority. However, Finn and his team emphasized the benefits of shared knowledge and the council's role as a mediator rather than a ruler.

Zara finally relented after witnessing the potential of the Enclave's medical technology. A portable medical unit capable of diagnosing and treating a range of illnesses impressed her and her people. "If this council truly represents mutual aid and not control, I will support it," Zara declared. "But I will hold you to your promises."

With the support of the major enclaves secured, the first official meeting of the Council of Enclaves was convened. Representatives from each enclave gathered in the neutral location, the large, abandoned community center. There was a palpable sense of hope and cautious optimism as they began to discuss the guidelines, protocols, and shared goals.

Oracle appeared, addressing the council. "The path you have chosen is one of cooperation and mutual benefit. By sharing knowledge and resources, you can build a future that honors the legacy of the Forgotten Enclave and ensures a better life for all."

Finn stood, addressing the council with a newfound confidence. "We have the tools, the knowledge, and the will to rebuild our world. Together, we can overcome the challenges ahead and create a future where our children can thrive. Let us use this opportunity wisely and honor the sacrifices of those who came before us."

The council's discussions were long and sometimes contentious, but gradually, they formed a cohesive plan. Guidelines for the ethical use of technology were established, protocols for sharing resources were agreed upon, and a system of accountability and transparency was put in place.

As the council adjourned, Finn felt a deep sense of accomplishment and hope. They had taken the first steps towards a new era of cooperation and rebuilding. The challenges ahead were immense, but with the support of the council and the unity of the enclaves, they had a real chance to create a better world.

And so, under the guidance of the Council of Enclaves and with the wisdom of Oracle, Finn and his companions set out to turn their vision into reality.

CHAPTER NINE

As the Council of Enclaves took shape, Oracle's presence became a guiding force in their deliberations. The AI's vast repository of knowledge and its commitment to ethical principles provided a foundation upon which the council could build. Oracle's suggestion to carefully select trustworthy leaders from various enclaves to share the knowledge responsibly resonated deeply with Finn.

One evening, as Finn, Lyra, Elias, and Elara gathered around the central console in the Enclave's command center, Oracle addressed them with a proposal. Its holographic form flickered with a calm, steady glow.

"Finn, you have demonstrated wisdom and integrity in your efforts to unite the enclaves," Oracle began. "However, to ensure the responsible dissemination of the Enclave's knowledge, it is essential to involve leaders who have shown a commitment to the greater good. I suggest a compromise: carefully selecting representatives from each enclave who have proven their dedication to peace and collaboration."

Finn nodded, his expression thoughtful. "I agree, Oracle. It's the best way to balance the risks and benefits. We need to ensure that this knowledge is used to rebuild, not to dominate."

Lyra, always pragmatic, added, "We'll need to establish criteria for selecting these leaders. They should be individuals who have shown not only leadership skills but also a genuine desire to help their communities."

Elias chimed in, "And we must ensure that the process is transparent and inclusive. Every enclave should have a voice in this decision."

Elara, her technical mind always working, suggested, "We can use the Enclave's communication systems to set up a secure network for this process. This way, each enclave can nominate and vote for their representatives without the need for risky travel."

With the plan set in motion, Finn and his team reached out to the enclaves once more, this time with a more focused mission. They explained Oracle's proposal and the need for carefully selected representatives. Each enclave was invited to nominate individuals who met the established criteria, and a secure voting process was put in place.

The response was encouraging. Leaders from various enclaves appreciated the emphasis on transparency and ethical considerations. Nominations poured in, and the secure network buzzed with activity as communities discussed and voted for their representatives.

After weeks of deliberation, the council reconvened, this time with a carefully chosen group of leaders. Each representative had been selected based on their wisdom, integrity, and commitment to the greater good. The atmosphere in the room was one of cautious optimism as they gathered to discuss the future.

Finn stood at the center of the room, addressing the newly formed council. "Thank you all for coming. Today marks the beginning of a new chapter. We have the knowledge and technology to rebuild, but we also have the responsibility to use it wisely. Together, we can create a future that honors the sacrifices of the past and ensures a better life for future generations."

The council members nodded in agreement, their expressions reflecting a mix of hope and determination. Elder Mira from Green Haven, Administrator Voss from the Technocrat's Enclave, and Zara from the Freehold were among the chosen representatives, each bringing their unique perspectives and strengths to the table.

Oracle's holographic form appeared, addressing the council with its calm, authoritative presence. "The journey ahead will be challenging, but with your collective wisdom and commitment, you can ensure that the Enclave's knowledge is used ethically and effectively. Let us begin by establishing the core principles that will guide our actions."

The council spent the next few days drafting a charter that outlined their shared goals and the ethical use of the Enclave's technology. They emphasized transparency, accountability, and the collective good, setting clear guidelines for the dissemination and application of the knowledge.

As the charter took shape, Oracle provided valuable insights, drawing on historical examples and ethical frameworks. The AI's vast repository of knowledge served as a valuable resource, helping the council navigate complex issues and potential pitfalls.

With the charter in place, the council turned its attention to practical matters. They discussed the immediate needs of their communities and how the Enclave's technology could address them. Priorities included clean energy, water purification, medical care, and sustainable agriculture.

Elder Mira spoke passionately about the need for clean water. "In Green Haven, we have managed to sustain ourselves through careful stewardship of our resources. But many communities still suffer from contaminated water sources. The portable water purifiers we have seen can make a significant difference."

Administrator Voss emphasized the importance of energy production. "The advanced reactors can provide a stable and renewable source of power. This is crucial for rebuilding infrastructure and supporting technological advancements."

Zara, ever the advocate for the underrepresented, highlighted the need for equitable access. "We must ensure that these technologies reach even the smallest and most isolated settlements. Everyone deserves a chance to benefit from this knowledge."

As the council worked through these issues, Finn felt a growing sense of pride and hope. They were not only addressing immediate needs but also laying the groundwork for a more cooperative and equitable future.

One evening, as the council adjourned for the day, Finn and Lyra stood on a balcony overlooking the settlement. The sun was setting, casting a warm, golden light over the landscape.

"We've come a long way," Lyra said, her voice filled with quiet admiration. "Seeing everyone work together like this, it's incredible."

Finn nodded, feeling a deep sense of fulfillment. "It is. We've faced so many challenges, but we've also found a way to unite and rebuild. I believe in what we're doing."

Lyra smiled, her eyes reflecting the setting sun. "And it's only the beginning. There's so much more to do, but with this council and the knowledge we've gained, we can make a real difference."

As night fell, the settlement lights flickered on, powered by the Enclave's advanced energy technology. Finn looked out over the scene, feeling a renewed sense of purpose. They had found a way to balance the risks and benefits, to share the Enclave's knowledge responsibly.

With the Council of Enclaves now established and a clear path forward, Finn knew that the journey ahead would still be filled with challenges. But he also knew that they had the wisdom, the determination, and the unity to overcome them.

And so, under the guidance of the Council and with Oracle's support, Finn and his companions continued their mission to rebuild and create a better future.

CHAPTER TEN

With the Council of Enclaves firmly established and a clear charter in place, it was time for the chosen leaders to visit the Forgotten Enclave. The objective was to select pieces of knowledge or technology that could immediately benefit their communities. Finn, understanding the importance of this pivotal moment, took on the responsibility of overseeing the process. He was determined to ensure that the Enclave's resources were used wisely and for the greater good.

The journey to the Enclave was a symbolic and practical gesture, signifying the unity and cooperative spirit that the Council embodied. Leaders from Green Haven, the Technocrat's Enclave, the Freehold, and other settlements made their way to the Enclave, each bringing a small delegation of trusted advisors and experts.

As they arrived, Finn greeted each leader personally, reaffirming the commitment to transparency and ethical use of the Enclave's technology. Elder Mira from Green Haven was the first to arrive, her serene presence bringing a sense of calm and purpose. Administrator Voss followed, his analytical mind already assessing the potential applications of the technology. Zara from the Freehold arrived with her characteristic energy, eager to explore the possibilities for her community.

The leaders and their delegations gathered in the Enclave's central chamber, where Oracle's holographic form welcomed them. "Welcome to the Forgotten Enclave," Oracle intoned, its voice steady and reassuring. "Today marks a significant step in our shared journey to rebuild and restore our world. Each of you will have the opportunity to select knowledge or technology that will benefit your communities. Let us begin."

Elder Mira stepped forward first, her eyes reflecting a deep sense of responsibility. "In Green Haven, we have always valued sustainable living. We need advanced agricultural techniques to improve our crop yields and ensure food security for our people."

Oracle displayed a series of holographic images and diagrams related to advanced farming methods, including hydroponics, aquaponics, and genetically modified crops designed to thrive in harsh conditions. Mira and her advisors studied the information carefully, selecting the techniques that would be most beneficial for their unique environment.

Administrator Voss was next. "Energy is our lifeblood. To rebuild infrastructure and support technological advancement, we need efficient and renewable energy sources."

Oracle presented blueprints for advanced energy reactors, detailing their design, operation, and maintenance. Voss's engineers were captivated by the potential of these reactors to provide clean, sustainable power. After thorough discussion and analysis, they chose a reactor design that could be implemented quickly and scaled to meet their needs.

Zara approached the console with a look of determination. "Medical care is essential for the well-being of our people. We need advanced medical technologies to address the many health challenges we face."

Oracle displayed an array of medical devices and treatments, from portable diagnostic units to advanced surgical tools and comprehensive vaccination programs. Zara's team, which included medics and health practitioners, selected technologies that would address immediate needs such as disease prevention and trauma care.

As each leader made their selections, Finn observed the process closely, ensuring that the technology was not only suited to their needs but also aligned with the ethical guidelines established by the Council. He worked with Oracle to provide additional insights and support, fostering a collaborative atmosphere.

Throughout the process, the leaders engaged in discussions, sharing their visions and concerns. The sense of mutual respect and shared purpose grew stronger, reinforcing the bonds that held the Council together.

Once the selections were finalized, the leaders prepared to return to their respective enclaves, each carrying a piece of the Enclave's knowledge that would help improve their communities. Finn gathered them one last time in the central chamber.

"Today, we have taken a significant step forward," Finn said, his voice filled with conviction. "The knowledge and technology you are taking back will help your communities, but it also represents something greater—a commitment to cooperation, ethical use, and the shared goal of rebuilding our world. Let us continue to work together, to support each other, and to ensure that this knowledge is used for the greater good."

Elder Mira nodded in agreement. "We have seen the potential of what we can achieve together. Let us honor this responsibility with wisdom and compassion."

Administrator Voss added, "Efficiency and mutual benefit must guide our actions. Together, we can overcome the challenges ahead."

Zara, always passionate, concluded, "This is just the beginning. Let's make sure that every community, no matter how small or isolated, benefits from what we've achieved here."

With that, the leaders departed, each returning to their enclaves with renewed hope and valuable resources. Finn remained at the Enclave, overseeing the continued operation and ensuring that the processes they had established were upheld.

The days that followed were filled with reports and updates from the various enclaves. Green Haven's crops flourished with the new agricultural techniques, providing an abundant harvest that fed not only their own people but also neighboring communities. The Technocrat's Enclave's new reactor provided stable, clean energy, powering their infrastructure and technological advancements. The Freehold's medical technologies improved health outcomes and saved countless lives, strengthening their community.

Finn took great pride in these successes but remained vigilant. He continued to work closely with Oracle, monitoring the implementation of the technologies and ensuring that the ethical guidelines were strictly followed. He knew that the true test of their efforts would be maintaining this balance of power and responsibility over the long term.

One evening, as Finn reviewed the latest reports, Oracle appeared beside him. "You have done well, Finn. The leaders you have chosen and the processes you have established are fostering a new era of cooperation and rebuilding."

Finn nodded, feeling a deep sense of fulfillment. "We still have a long way to go, but we've made a good start. It's incredible to see the positive changes already happening."

Oracle's holographic form flickered slightly. "Remember, Finn, the journey is ongoing. There will always be challenges and temptations. But with the Council's commitment to ethical use and mutual support, you can continue to build a future that honors the legacy of the Forgotten Enclave."

Finn stood, looking out over the settlement, the lights of the Enclave glowing in the distance. "We'll face whatever comes, together. And we'll keep working to create a world that's better for everyone."

CHAPTER ELEVEN

As the enclaves began to implement the technologies and knowledge they had acquired, a transformation took place across the region. The collaborative efforts fostered by the Council of Enclaves led to significant improvements in living conditions, health, and infrastructure. The spirit of cooperation grew stronger, with each enclave contributing its strengths and sharing its resources for the common good.

Green Haven, with its advanced agricultural techniques, became a vital food supplier for the other enclaves. The abundant harvests fed not only their own people but also neighboring communities, alleviating hunger and fostering goodwill. The Technocrat's Enclave, with its expertise in energy production, provided stable, renewable power that fueled the rebuilding efforts. The Freehold's medical advancements improved health outcomes across the board, reducing disease and increasing life expectancy.

Regular communication between the enclaves became the norm, facilitated by the Enclave's advanced communication systems. Leaders and representatives met frequently to discuss progress, address challenges, and share new discoveries. The Council of Enclaves emerged as a powerful symbol of unity and hope, guiding the region towards a more prosperous and peaceful future.

Finn's role in these developments did not go unnoticed. He was recognized not only for his discovery of the Forgotten Enclave but also for his wisdom and leadership in managing its secrets. People from all enclaves began to see him as a hero, a figure who had brought them together and shown them the path to a better future.

One sunny afternoon, the Council of Enclaves convened in Green Haven to celebrate the successes achieved so far and to plan the next steps in their collective journey. The large communal hall was filled with representatives from each enclave, their faces reflecting a mix of pride and determination.

Elder Mira, acting as the host, addressed the assembly. "We have come a long way since our first meeting. The progress we have made is a testament to our commitment to cooperation and mutual support. Today, we celebrate our achievements and look forward to the future."

Administrator Voss stood and spoke next. "The energy reactors have provided a stable power source, enabling us to rebuild our infrastructure and support technological advancements. But we must remain vigilant and continue to innovate, ensuring that our systems are efficient and sustainable."

Zara from the Freehold added, "Our medical technologies have saved countless lives and improved health outcomes across the region. We must continue to share this knowledge and ensure that every community, no matter how small, has access to quality healthcare."

Elder Mira then turned to Finn, who sat modestly among the other representatives. "And now, we recognize the individual whose vision and leadership have made all this possible. Finn, please come forward."

Finn, slightly taken aback, stood and walked to the front of the hall. He looked out at the assembled leaders and representatives, feeling a deep sense of gratitude and humility.

Elder Mira continued, "Finn, you have not only discovered the Forgotten Enclave but also guided us with wisdom and integrity. Your efforts have united our communities and set us on a path to a brighter future. For this, we recognize you as a true hero and a guiding light for our people."

The hall erupted in applause, the sound echoing off the walls. Finn felt a lump in his throat as he looked around at the faces of those he had come to respect and admire. He raised his hand to quiet the crowd, then spoke with heartfelt sincerity.

"Thank you, Elder Mira, and thank you to all of you. I am deeply honored by your recognition, but I must emphasize that this success is not mine alone. It belongs to all of us—every leader, every representative, every person who has worked tirelessly to rebuild and improve our lives. The true heroes are the people who come together, who share their knowledge and resources, and who are committed to building a better future for everyone."

He paused, allowing his words to sink in. "We have made incredible progress, but our journey is far from over. There will be challenges ahead, and we must face them with the same spirit of cooperation and unity that has brought us this far. Together, we can overcome any obstacle and continue to build a society that reflects our highest ideals."

The applause was even louder this time, and Finn felt a profound sense of connection to the people in the room. He knew that their collective efforts would shape the future in ways that went beyond his initial vision.

As the meeting continued, the Council discussed plans for further collaboration and innovation. They explored new areas of research, from environmental restoration to advanced education systems, all aimed at creating a sustainable and thriving society.

In the weeks and months that followed, the enclaves worked more closely than ever. Joint projects were launched, combining the expertise and resources of multiple communities. Engineers from the Technocrat's Enclave collaborated with farmers from Green Haven to develop automated irrigation systems. Medical professionals from the Freehold traveled to remote settlements, providing training and support to local health workers.

Finn remained at the heart of these efforts, working tirelessly to ensure that the Enclave's knowledge was used responsibly and for the greater good. He continued to meet with leaders, mediate disputes, and inspire those around him with his unwavering commitment to their shared vision.

One evening, as Finn walked through the bustling streets of the settlement, he reflected on how far they had come. The lights from the Enclave's advanced reactors illuminated the night, casting a warm glow over the community. He passed by a clinic where patients received state-of-the-art medical care, a field where crops flourished under the guidance of new agricultural techniques, and a school where children learned about the wonders of science and technology.

Finn knew that there would always be challenges and uncertainties, but he also knew that they had built a strong foundation based on trust, cooperation, and a shared commitment to the greater good. The future was bright, and he was grateful to be a part of it.

As he looked up at the stars, Finn felt a deep sense of peace and fulfillment. The wasteland was still a harsh and dangerous place, but within its desolate embrace, the spark of hope had grown into a beacon of light. And as long as that light shone, there was the promise of a better tomorrow for all.

The journey of rebuilding and uniting the enclaves was far from over, but with the wisdom of the Council, the guidance of Oracle, and the unwavering spirit of the people, Finn knew that they would continue to rise above the challenges and create a future that honored the legacy of the past and embraced the possibilities of the future.

EPILOGUE

As the sun dipped below the horizon, casting a warm golden light over the settlement, Finn made his way back to the Enclave. The once-hidden sanctuary had become a bustling hub of activity and innovation, a symbol of hope and progress for all the enclaves. Finn walked through the Enclave's corridors, reflecting on the remarkable journey that had brought them here.

He remembered the first time he had stepped into the Enclave, awestruck by the advanced technology and the wealth of knowledge it contained. He had felt a profound sense of responsibility, knowing that the decisions he made would shape the future. Now, as he looked around at the thriving community, he felt a deep sense of pride and fulfillment.

Reaching the central chamber, Finn found Oracle waiting for him. The AI's holographic form flickered to life, its presence a comforting constant in the ever-changing world.

"Welcome back, Finn," Oracle said, its voice filled with warmth. "You have achieved much since you first arrived here. The progress you and the Council have made is truly remarkable."

Finn smiled, feeling a wave of gratitude. "Thank you, Oracle. We couldn't have done it without your guidance and support. The Enclave has given us the tools we needed to rebuild, but it's the people—their spirit and determination—that have made this possible."

Oracle nodded. "Indeed. The true strength of humanity lies not in its technology, but in its ability to come together, to cooperate and support one another. You have harnessed that strength and used it to create a brighter future."

As Finn looked around the chamber, he felt a sense of peace and contentment. But he also knew that their journey was far from over. "We've come a long way, but there are still many challenges ahead. The world is slowly healing, but there's so much more we need to do."

Oracle's form shimmered slightly, as if considering Finn's words. "The path to recovery is long and fraught with difficulties. There will be new challenges and opportunities, and it is crucial that you remain vigilant and committed to the principles that have guided you thus far."

Finn nodded, understanding the weight of Oracle's words. "We need to continue fostering cooperation and ethical use of technology. We can't let greed or ambition undermine what we've built."

"Precisely," Oracle agreed. "The knowledge contained within the Enclave is powerful, but it must be used wisely. You and the Council must continue to lead with integrity, ensuring that this knowledge benefits all and does not become a tool for exploitation."

Finn thought about the future and the possibilities that lay ahead. "What do you see as our next steps, Oracle? How can we continue to build on what we've achieved?"

Oracle's holographic form shifted, displaying images of new technologies and potential projects. "There are many avenues to explore. Environmental restoration, for example, is critical. Rebuilding ecosystems and restoring natural resources will ensure long-term sustainability. Advanced education systems will empower the next generation to continue this work. And we must also consider ways to improve infrastructure and transportation, connecting communities and fostering further collaboration."

Finn felt a surge of excitement as he envisioned the possibilities. "We can do this. With the Council's support and the commitment of our people, we can continue to make progress and create a better world."

Oracle's form stabilized, its voice filled with optimism. "I believe in your vision, Finn. You have shown that humanity has the capacity for greatness, even in the face of adversity. Together, you can overcome any challenge and seize the opportunities that lie ahead."

As the night deepened, Finn and Oracle continued to discuss plans and ideas for the future. They talked about new projects, potential alliances with other communities, and ways to ensure that the Enclave's knowledge was preserved and expanded. Finn felt a renewed sense of purpose, knowing that there was still much work to be done.

Finally, as the first light of dawn began to filter into the chamber, Finn stood and stretched. "Thank you, Oracle. Your guidance has been invaluable, and I look forward to continuing this journey together."

Oracle's form shimmered with a soft glow. "Thank you, Finn. It has been an honor to support you and the Council. I will continue to be here, ready to assist in any way I can."

With a final nod, Finn left the central chamber, stepping out into the fresh morning air. The settlement was coming to life, with people going about their daily tasks, their faces filled with hope and determination. Finn took a deep breath, feeling the warmth of the sun on his face, and smiled.

He walked through the streets, greeting friends and neighbors, feeling a deep connection to the community they had built together. As he looked around at the thriving settlement, he knew that the journey was far from over, but he also knew that they were on the right path.

The challenges ahead were daunting, but Finn felt confident that they could overcome them. With the support of the Council, the wisdom of Oracle, and the unwavering spirit of the people, they would continue to rebuild and create a better future for all.

And so, Finn continued his work, leading with integrity and compassion, always mindful of the responsibility that came with the Enclave's knowledge. He knew that the world was slowly healing, and with each step forward, they were creating a legacy of hope, progress, and unity.

The wasteland was still a harsh and dangerous place, but within its desolate embrace, the spark of hope had grown into a beacon of light. And as long as that light shone, there was the promise of a brighter tomorrow for all.